Nicked!

by

David Belbin

Illustrated by Liz McIntosh

For everyone at Rushcliffe Comp.
1985-1994

First published in Great Britain by Barrington Stoke Ltd
10 Belford Terrace, Edinburgh, EH4 3DQ
Copyright © 1999 David Belbin
Illustrations © Liz McIntosh
The moral right of the author has been asserted in
accordance with the Copyright, Designs and
Patents Act 1988
ISBN 1-902260-29-5
Printed by Polestar AUP Aberdeen Ltd

MEET THE AUTHOR - DAVID BELBIN

What is your favourite animal?
Cats (but I can't have one because my girlfriend's allergic to them)
What is your favourite boy's name?
Harry
What is your favourite girl's name?
Rachel
What is your favourite food?
Monkfish
What is your favourite music?
What's The Frequency Kenneth?
by REM
What is your favourite hobby?
Collecting American comics like
Stray Bullets and *Optic Nerve*

MEET THE ILLUSTRATOR - LIZ MCINTOSH

What is your favourite animal?
Horses
What is your favourite boy's name?
Thomas
What is your favourite girl's name?
Edith
What is your favourite food?
Cake
What is your favourite music?
Abba
What is your favourite hobby?
Reading, drawing and eating cake

Barrington Stoke was a famous and much-loved story-teller. He travelled from village to village carrying a lantern to light his way. He arrived as it grew dark and when the young boys and girls of the village saw the glow of his lantern, they hurried to the central meeting place. They were full of excitement and expectation, for his stories were always wonderful.

Then Barrington Stoke set down his lantern. In the flickering light the listeners were enthralled by his tales of adventure, horror and mystery. He knew exactly what they liked best and he loved telling a good story. And another. And then another. When the lantern burned low and dawn was nearly breaking, he slipped away. He was gone by morning, only to appear the next day in some other village to tell the next story.

Contents

Prologue

The footsteps drew nearer. They were coming. Nick Hooper could hear two people talking, but couldn't make out what they were saying. He had nowhere to hide. There was no one to help him – only the cleaners were left. Smith School had been closed for an hour.

Nick should never have done what he did, but now it was too late. He had to hide the tape, but where should he put it? The footsteps sounded louder in the long corridor outside. Nick knew who had sent them and why. He could run for it, but what was the point?

Wait. He had an idea. Nick tried the door of the big store cupboard at the back of the classroom. This was where Mr Fisher, the Media Studies teacher, kept all the television and video stuff. The door was unlocked. That was odd. Mr Fisher must have been in a hurry and forgotten to lock it.

Nick turned on the light. There was a row of Video 8 tapes on a high shelf. Nick took one out of its box. He swapped one of the tiny Video 8 cassettes with another from the pocket of his fleece. Maybe he would get away with it.

Nick heard their voices right outside the classroom door. Should he stay in the cupboard? No. They were bound to find him. He turned off the light and went back into the classroom. He hung his fleece on the back of a chair. As he sat down, the door opened.

Chapter 1
Clueless

Detective Inspector Dudden drove into Smith School at 5.11 p.m. It was early winter and just starting to get dark. The policeman hurried to Mr Fisher's classroom. Tall, pretty Community Constable Carpenter was waiting in the corridor outside the room.

"I did what you said, Sir," she said. "I've locked all three of them in the classroom."

"How old are they?" Inspector Dudden asked.

"They're aged about fifteen or sixteen," the constable replied.

There was a small window in the door. The inspector looked through it. He saw three youths. Two of them were wearing dark puffa jackets. The other was in shirt sleeves, even though the school heating had been turned off.

All three boys looked shifty, Inspector Dudden thought. One had black hair. One had red hair. The one in shirt sleeves had blonde hair. What were they doing here? The inspector was sure of one thing. There had been several thefts from this room. One or more of these boys was behind them.

"Have you rung Mr Fisher?" the inspector asked Constable Carpenter. "After all, this is his classroom."

"Yes, Sir. But there was nobody home. I left a message on his answering machine, asking him to come in."

"I see," said the inspector. "The trouble is we won't know if anything's missing."

"Unless we find it on them, Sir."

"That's true," Inspector Dudden said, "but they've had plenty of time to put things back. Oh well, let's go and have a word with them."

Constable Carpenter unlocked the door. The room looked like there had been a fight in it. Tables and chairs had been tipped over. There was a blood stain on the teacher's desk.

"Do you know any of these boys?" Inspector Dudden asked Constable Carpenter.

"I'm afraid not, Sir," she said. "None of them has been in trouble on my patch."

Inspector Dudden looked carefully at them. The blonde boy was the tallest. He had crooked teeth and a bloody nose. This did not make him a villain, but it made him look like one.

The red-haired boy had a bruise on his cheek, but that did not make him the victim, either. He could have started a fight, then got hurt himself.

The black-haired boy was the most heavily built. He had a bloody nose too. The inspector decided to pick on him first. He took the boy out into the corridor.

"What's your name?" he asked the black-haired boy.

"Nick Hopper," the boy replied.

"Do you go to this school?" the inspector asked.

"Yes, Sir," the black-haired boy said.

"And what are you doing here?" Inspector Dudden asked.

"Mr Fisher put me in detention," the youth explained.

"What for?"

"Losing equipment, Sir."

"And where is Mr Fisher?" the inspector asked.

"He never showed up, Sir," the boy explained. "But I waited here anyway. You don't miss Mr Fisher's detentions. Everyone's terrified of him."

"I see," said the inspector. "And what are these other boys doing here?"

"I don't know, Sir. They showed up and started throwing things around. I tried to stop them. The tall lad gave me this nosebleed."

"Do you know who they are?" Inspector Dudden asked.

"No. I don't think they even go to this school!"

"All right. Thank you, Nick."

Next the inspector sent for the red-haired boy with the bruised face.

"What's your name, son?"

The red-haired boy gave him a confident look. "Nick Hopper," he said.

Inspector Dudden looked at Constable Carpenter.

"Things are getting interesting," she said. "This is quite a coincidence, two of you sharing the same name."

The second Nick Hopper told the same tale as the first one. He was doing a detention when two boys charged in and started a fight.

"Have you any proof of your identity?" Inspector Dudden asked.

"I'm afraid not, Sir. I forgot my bag today."

"All right, go back to the classroom and send out the third boy," the inspector said.

"And what about you?" the inspector asked the tall, blonde-haired boy with the crooked teeth and no coat. "Do you have a name?"

"I'd rather not say," the blonde boy said. He looked worried.

"Perhaps you're called Nick Hopper too," the inspector said, sarcastically.

The boy didn't reply. He was probably the thief, Inspector Dudden decided. But which of the other two boys was his mate? Or were they both innocent? They couldn't both be called Nick Hopper, could they?

The inspector turned to Constable Carpenter. "This puts us in a difficult position," he said. "Before we take them to the station, we really ought to call their parents."

"I agree," Constable Carpenter said. "Perhaps we should see if they have any proof of identity on them."

"Good idea," the inspector said.

The two officers went into the classroom. The lads sat as far apart from each other as they could.

"All right," the inspector said. "Turn out your pockets."

The black-haired boy did as he was told. In his pockets he had a penknife, a house key,

some scrunched up tissue and one piece of chewing gum. There was nothing with his name on it.

"Now you," Constable Carpenter said to the redhead.

The red-haired boy also emptied out his pockets. He had some polo mints, a key ring with two keys on it, and a small ballpoint. Again, there was nothing with his name on it.

"Now you," the inspector said to the blonde boy. "Let's see what you've got on you."

But the blonde boy's trouser pockets were empty.

"Where's your coat?" Constable Carpenter asked him.

"On the back of that chair," the blonde boy said. He pointed at the brown fleece.

Inspector Dudden went over and checked the pockets. There was no bus pass in it. No keys, either. This boy was a real mystery. But there *was* something. Was it cigarettes?

"What's this?" he said, pulling out a tiny plastic box.

He looked at the Video 8 tape, hoping that it would be labelled. There was nothing written on it.

"I wonder," the inspector said, "whether we can see what's on this. Where would I find a video player?"

He looked from the first boy to the second boy to the third boy. Finally, the blonde boy cracked.

"You can play it on one of the video cameras in that store cupboard over there," he said, pointing at a green door.

"How do you know that it's a store cupboard?" Constable Carpenter asked.

"I have lessons in this classroom," the blonde boy said.

"What was your name again?" Constable Carpenter asked, sneakily.

The blonde boy didn't reply.

"Maybe there's a name in your fleece," Constable Carpenter said.

She picked it up and looked inside. There was no name. However, as she lifted the fleece, she felt something moving about. It was in the same pocket where the inspector had found the video tape.

"What's this?" she asked. She pulled out something cold, heavy and metallic. "A magnet!"

Constable Carpenter handed the item to Inspector Dudden.

"I suppose you think you've been very clever," Inspector Dudden said to the blonde boy. "The magnet will have erased whatever was on this tape."

The blonde boy shrugged his shoulders and replied, "Somebody thinks they've been clever."

"And you still won't tell us your name?" Constable Carpenter asked.

"You wouldn't believe me," the blonde boy said.

Constable Carpenter and Inspector Dudden looked at each other.

"Where do we go from here?" the inspector wanted to know.

The three lads sat waiting for their decision.

"Why don't we make them sweat?" the constable whispered to her boss.

"Good idea," the inspector whispered back. Then he added, in a loud voice, "Do any of you want to call your parents to tell them you'll be late?"

None of the boys took up his offer.

"There's only one thing for it," Inspector Dudden told Constable Carpenter. "I'm going to get the headteacher. She can sort this out."

The inspector went to the door.

"Don't let this lot out of your sight," he told Constable Carpenter.

Chapter 2
Who's Who?

The three boys sat on the tables in the cold room, not looking at each other. The real Nick wondered how he was going to get out of this. Constable Carpenter seemed OK. Maybe if he could get her on her own ... but he wasn't sure that he could convince her of the truth. Things were too confusing.

Nick hadn't expected to have his name stolen. That made things more complicated. The other two boys had tried to beat him up. They'd warned him that something worse would happen if he didn't hand over the tape. If Constable Carpenter hadn't arrived in time, Nick would have been badly hurt. He wanted to tell Constable Carpenter the truth. But what was the point? It was safest to wait.

*****

Constable Carpenter looked at the three boys. The blonde one with the crooked teeth was chewing his fingernails. He would be the first to crack, she decided.

"You might as well tell me now," she said. "Inspector Dudden's gone off to fetch somebody who can identify you all."

The black-haired boy (who she thought of as Nick One) looked fed up.

"Isn't it about time you let us go?" he asked. "I'll be late for my tea."

"Give us your phone number and I'll warn your Mum," Constable Carpenter told him.

"You've got no right to hold us here," the red-haired boy (Nick Two) said.

"That's as maybe, if you give me your home address, we'll drop you off there in a little while," Constable Carpenter said. "Otherwise,

23

I'll assume that you've got no home to go to. So I'll keep you here for your own protection."

Nick One and Nick Two sneered at her. *Which of them was the fake?* she wondered. Why was one pretending to be the other? Constable Carpenter wasn't a detective, but she knew a few things about criminals. Most of them were very stupid. A few thought that they were clever. They tended to be even more stupid.

Which of these three boys had set off the alarm in the store cupboard? It was a secret alarm. Even the class teacher, Mr Fisher, didn't know about it.

Only the headteacher and the police knew it was there.

The alarm had been the headteacher's idea. It was connected directly to the police station. The Head, Mrs Roser, was dead keen to find out who kept stealing the school's audio-visual equipment.

Three video recorders, four video cameras and a mixing desk had gone in the last few months. The school's insurance premiums were going sky high. Who was responsible? It had to be one of Mr Fisher's Media Studies students. But how had they done it? There had never been any sign of a break-in.

"I've had enough," the red-haired boy said. "I'm going."

"Me too," the black-haired boy said. "You've got no right to hold us."

They both got off their tables and stood in front of Constable Carpenter. They looked like they were going to barge past her. Constable Carpenter reached out and grabbed both of them by the collars of their jackets.

"You're not going anywhere," she said.

"We might not be," Nick One said. "But he is."

Constable Carpenter looked over his shoulder. The blonde boy had grabbed his fleece from the back of the chair.

"Catch you later!" he shouted, and swerved past her, out of the door.

"Come back!" Constable Carpenter yelled.

You stupid cow! she called herself. *Why hadn't she locked the door when the inspector left?* But it was too late. The blonde boy had gone.

A minute later, Inspector Dudden returned with Mrs Roser.

"Where's the kid with no name?" the inspector asked.

Constable Carpenter, embarrassed, explained what had happened. Mrs Roser was understanding.

"Strictly speaking," she said, "we can't keep anybody after school without their parents' permission. Now, who are these two?"

"We were hoping that you'd be able to tell us that," Inspector Dudden said.

"They don't look very familiar," Mrs Roser said. "What did you say your names were?" she asked the two boys.

"Nick Hopper," they said in chorus.

"And whose class are you in?"

"Mr Fisher's," said the black-haired boy, Nick One.

"And why are you here?" the headteacher asked the second Nick.

"Detention," the red-haired boy said.

"Where's your detention form?" Mrs Roser wanted to know. "Come on, I want to see what Mr Fisher wrote."

"Is that it?" Constable Carpenter said, pointing at a pink form on the teacher's desk.

"Yes." The Head picked it up and read aloud, "*Nick is behind with his course work and has used the school video equipment without permission.* Which of you would care to explain this?"

Neither boy said anything.

"It would he helpful," Constable Carpenter told Mrs Roser, "if you could tell us which of these boys is the real Nick Hopper."

"I wish I could," the Head said. "But, to be honest, I don't recognise either of them. This is a big school, and ..."

She didn't finish her sentence. Constable Carpenter had another idea.

"Is there a photograph in Nick's file?" she asked.

"Normally, there would be," Mrs Roser said. "I checked Nick Hopper's file before coming over here. The trouble is, he moved here halfway through Year Eight. That was long after the photos were taken. So we only have his home address and phone number."

"Why don't you try ringing his parents?" Inspector Dudden suggested. "They can tell us whether their son has dark hair or ginger hair. Then we'll be a little nearer solving this mystery."

"Good idea," Mrs Roser said. "I'll go and call now."

"While you're at it," Constable Carpenter said, "maybe you could see if Mr Fisher's home yet."

"Of course," Mrs Roser said. "He ought to he able to shed some light on this situation."

She hurried out of the classroom. Inspector Dudden blocked the door.

"Don't either of you even think of trying to run away again," he said.

The two Nicks sat back down on the tables. They didn't look at each other. Nick One seemed angry with Nick Two, Constable Carpenter thought. Why was that? Which of them had tried to break into the store cupboard?

The Head returned.

"There's nobody in at Nick's and Mr Fisher's not back yet," she said.

"You'd better let us go," Nick Two said.

"Yeah, you can't keep us forever," Nick One pointed out.

"Hold on," Constable Carpenter said. "I've got an idea."

Chapter 3
The Truth

Ten minutes later, a police car drew up outside Nick Hopper's house. Large lime trees shaded the small semi. The two boys sat in the back with Inspector Dudden.

"We don't want anyone else running off on us," he said.

The two Nick Hoppers got out of the car.
They were whispering to each other. Constable
Carpenter couldn't make out everything they
said. She was pretty sure what the big one was
whispering, though.

"It's all your fault," Nick One was telling
Nick Two.

Curtains twitched and blinds rustled all
along the street. The neighbours wanted to
know what the police were doing there.

"Get out your key," Inspector Dudden told
Nick One.

"It won't fit," the lad said, angrily.

"Why's that, then?" the inspector asked.

"Because it's the key to my bike lock," Nick
One replied. "I don't have a key to the house."

He handed the key to the inspector. He was right, it was the wrong kind of key.

"And where's your bike?" the inspector wanted to know.

"Back at the school," Nick One said.

"You'll have a bit of a walk then, won't you?" Constable Carpenter pointed out. She turned to the other boy. "All right, let's see your keys!"

Reluctantly, Nick Two put a hand into his pocket. *He must be the real Nick*, Constable Carpenter decided. Maybe some of the stolen stuff was inside the house.

Nick Two handed his key ring to Inspector Dudden. The inspector was fitting a key into the lock when the front door burst open.

"What the ...?" An angry-looking woman was glaring at them. "Who the heck do you think you are?" she demanded. Then she spotted Constable Carpenter.

"I'm sorry," the constable said. "We didn't think that anybody was home."

"So I can see," said Mrs Hopper. "What's going on?"

Inspector Dudden took over. "We need to know one thing," he said. "Which of these boys is your son?"

Mrs Hopper looked confused.

"*My son*!" she said. "Why, neither of them. My Nick's upstairs. He got home ten minutes ago, just after I got back from the childminders. NICK!" she yelled, "COME DOWN HERE!"

A moment later, they heard footsteps on the stairs. The tall, blonde boy with crooked teeth appeared in the hallway. He looked embarrassed.

"Looks like we've caught you, my lad," Inspector Dudden said.

"What's going on?" Mrs Hopper wanted to know.

"There's been a bit of a misunderstanding,"
the real Nick said.

"Why didn't you tell us your real name?"
Constable Carpenter asked him.

"Because you wouldn't have believed me, not
after these two both pretended to be me," Nick
explained. "I was sitting near the door, so I could

hear what they said. First they came in and tried to beat me up, then they pretended to be me!"

On the path, Nick One began to kick Nick Two. "This wouldn't have happened if you hadn't copied me!" he said. "Idiot!"

"I didn't hear what you said!" the red-haired boy complained. "I didn't know what game you were playing. Nick Hopper was the only name I could think of!"

"Will someone tell me what this is all about?" Mrs Hopper demanded.

Inspector Dudden explained.

Mrs Hopper turned to the real Nick. "Have you been stealing equipment?" she asked.

"No. Of course not!"

"You had that video camera at the weekend," Mrs Hopper pointed out. "You said you had permission to borrow it."

"I did, from Mr Fisher. Only he didn't know what I really wanted to borrow it for."

"What *did* you want to borrow it for?" Constable Carpenter asked.

"To catch the thieves who've been stealing stuff from our school," Nick explained. "Everybody in our Media Studies class is behind with their work because people keep stealing the equipment."

"And how did you hope to catch them?" Inspector Dudden asked.

"Easy," Nick said. "Everybody knows that dodgy stuff gets sold in the car park of the *Coach and Horses*. So I went and staked it out on Saturday night."

43

Nick One and Nick Two began to look worried.

"I hung around for hours," the real Nick explained. "Then I saw these two idiots getting electrical gear out of the boot of a car. They handed the stuff over to someone."

"This proves nothing," Nick One said, angrily. "He's making things up."

"I'm not," Nick said. "I videoed it. The film's shadowy, but I'll bet you can make out that it's you two."

"We'll see about that," Inspector Dudden said. "Where's the tape?"

"It's at school," Nick said.

"I think you'll find that someone put a magnet next to it," Constable Carpenter pointed out. "If you remember they were both in your pocket. Magnets distort video tapes. The picture's probably no good."

"I switched the video tapes when I heard these two coming," Nick said. "I went into the storeroom and took a blank tape from there. The original's on the top shelf."

Inspector Dudden grinned and turned to the Head. "It looks like we have the vital evidence, Mrs Roser," he said.

The Head smiled. "It's lucky you went into the storeroom, Nick. You see, we had an alarm installed in there at the weekend. It alerted the police that there was a break-in. That's why they got to you before these two could finish beating you up."

"I was fighting them off pretty well, thank you," Nick said.

"But what I don't understand is this," the Head said, thinking aloud. "Why was the storeroom door open?"

"Mr Fisher left it unlocked," Nick said. "He left the room while I was in detention and never came back."

"But why were you in detention?" the Head asked him.

"Mr Fisher said it was because I was seen in the car park with a video camera. He lent me the camera himself. The condition was that I only used it at home."

"I should hope so too," said Mrs Roser. "We can't have people taking school equipment to dodgy places where it might be stolen."

Nick frowned. Mrs Roser realised what she'd said and blushed.

"But what happened to Mr Fisher?" Constable Carpenter asked. "Where did he get to?"

"That's what I'd like to know," Nick said.

All five people turned to the two fake Nicks.

"No idea," Nick One said.

"I don't even know what he looks like," Nick Two said.

"That's right," Nick One confirmed. "We don't even go to Smith School."

"Well, you're going back there now," Inspector Dudden said.

Chapter 4
Guilty!

All six people squeezed into the police car (Nick's Mum stayed behind because she had to look after his brother and sister). A message came on the police radio.

"There's been another break-in at the school," it said.

They drove into the school car park with sirens blaring. Constable Carpenter had to drag

the two fake Nicks along behind her. When they got to the classroom, it appeared to be empty. But the door to the video cupboard was open. There was a rattling noise inside.

"Police! Come out of there, whoever you are!" called Inspector Dudden.

A man in his mid-twenties appeared from the cupboard. It was Mr Fisher. His fierce face now looked sheepish. He turned from Inspector Dudden to Constable Carpenter to the real Nick to Nick One to Nick Two and finally to Mrs Roser.

"What are you doing back at school?" the Head asked.

"There was a message on my answering machine," Mr Fisher said. "It sounded like there was a problem."

"Yes," Mrs Roser said. "There is a problem." She pointed at the two fake Nicks. "Do you know these boys?"

"No," Mr Fisher said. "I've never seen either of them before."

"But you know this boy," she said, pointing at the real Nick.

"Oh yes, I had him in detention."

"Why did you leave him here, unattended?" Mrs Roser asked.

"I didn't," Mr Fisher said. "I told him to go. He can't have heard me."

That's not true, Nick thought, but he didn't say anything. He was beginning to suspect what had really happened.

"Why did you leave the video cupboard door unlocked?" Inspector Dudden asked.

"Was it unlocked?" Mr Fisher asked. "If it was, that must have been a mistake," he admitted. "When I got the message on the answering machine, I thought there had been another robbery. That's why I hurried back."

"Is anything missing?" the Head asked.

"Not as far as I can see," Mr Fisher said.

"Good. Please set up a video and TV for us."

"Why?" Mr Fisher asked.

"Just do as I say, please," Mrs Roser said.

Mr Fisher went and got the TV out. While he was connecting the video camera, Mrs Roser took Nick into the stock cupboard.

"Is the tape still here?" she asked him.

Nick went through the tapes on the top shelf.

"I put it in the box the wrong way round," he told the Head. "So I think this is it."

As the tape went into the machine, the other two boys looked worried. On the telly, there was a dark pub car park. A white Golf had its boot open. Two people were taking things out of it. They looked just like Nick One and Nick Two.

"Freeze frame the picture!" Inspector Dudden said, then cursed. "I can only make out the first two letters of the car's number plate."

Suddenly, Nick realised something. While everybody else was watching the video, he slipped out of the room. Nick hurried to the car park. There were only three cars in it. One was the Head's. One was the police car. The other was a white Golf.

When he got back to the classroom, Inspector Dudden was yelling at the two fake Nicks.

"Which of you stole the stuff? Was it both of you? How did you know to find Nick here, after school? AND WHAT ARE YOUR REAL NAMES?"

But the boys were both silent.

"I think I know what happened," Nick said.

Everybody turned to him.

"These two didn't steal the video equipment," Nick announced. "They don't go to this school. I watched them in the *Coach and Horses* car park. They were selling all sorts – smuggled cigarettes, dodgy perfume, stereo stuff. I reckon that they bought the video equipment from the real thief."

"And who's that?" Mrs Roser asked.

Nick explained. "The real thief told these two thugs that I'd be here. The idea was that they would beat me up and get the tape out of me. The thief drives a white Golf which is in the car park now. The first letters of his number plate are ..."

Before Nick could finish the sentence, Mr Fisher jumped to his feet and began to run.

He didn't get very far. Inspector Dudden stuck his foot out and the teacher went flying. Mr Fisher twisted his ankle as he fell, then banged his head on the wall. The two police officers picked him up.

"I suspected him all along," Mrs Roser said, as Constable Carpenter handcuffed Mr Fisher. "That's why I didn't tell him about the alarm on the video store cupboard. But why did he leave it unlocked? The police wouldn't have come if he'd locked it."

"I reckon he took some more stuff and meant to frame me for the robbery," Nick told her.

"You could be right," Inspector Dudden said. "We'll get a search warrant for his house. Well done, Nick."

"Your mother will be worried," Mrs Roser told Nick. "If the police are finished with us, I'll give you a lift home."

"That's fine," Inspector Dudden said. "We'll take your statements in the morning. But, as for you three ..." He looked at the two fake Nicks and Mr Fisher with a fierce grin, "You're nick-nick-nicked."

 Other Barrington Stoke titles available:-

What's Going On, Gus? by Jill Atkins 1-902260-10-4
Bungee Hero by Julie Bertagna 1-902260-23-6
Hostage by Malorie Blackman 1-902260-12-0
The Two Jacks by Tony Bradman 1-902260-30-9
Starship Rescue by Theresa Breslin 1-902260-24-4
Ghost for Sale by Terry Deary 1-902260-14-7
Sam the Detective by Terrance Dicks 1-902260-19-8
Billy the Squid by Colin Dowland 1-902260-04-X
Eddie and the Zedlines by Colin Dowland 1-902260-31-7
Kick Back by Vivian French 1-902260-02-3
The Gingerbread House by Adèle Geras 1-902260-03-1
Danny's Great Goal by Michael Hardcastle 1-902260-32-5
Ship of Ghosts by Nigel Hinton 1-902260-33-3
Virtual Friend by Mary Hoffman 1-902260-00-7
The Genie by Mary Hooper 1-902260-20-1
Tod in Biker City by Anthony Masters 1-902260-15-5
Wartman by Michael Morpurgo 1-902260-05-8
Whirlwind by Judith O'Neill 1-902260-34-1
Extra Time by Jenny Oldfield 1-902260-13-9
Screw Loose by Alison Prince 1-902260-01-5
Life Line by Rosie Rushton 1-902260-21-X
Problems with a Python by Jeremy Strong 1-902260-22-8
Lift Off by Hazel Townson 1-902260-11-2

Barrington Stoke, 10 Belford Terrace, Edinburgh EH4 3DQ
Tel: 0131 315 4933 Fax: 0131 315 4934
E-mail: info@barringtonstoke.co.uk
Website: www.barringtonstoke.co.uk